USE OF LAND

BARBARA JAMES

Thomson Learning • New York

Young Geographer

The Changing Earth
Food and Farming
Journeys
Natural Resources
Protecting the Planet
Settlements
Transportation
Use of Land
The World's Population
The World's Weather

Front cover: Harvesting wheat in Minnesota.
Back cover: Land-based oil rig in a pine forest,
Oklahoma.
Frontispiece: Planting rice in the flooded terraces of a rice paddy
near Bali, Indonesia.

First published in the
United States in 1993 by
Thomson Learning
115 Fifth Avenue
New York, NY 10003

First published in 1993 by
Wayland (Publishers) Ltd.

Cataloging-in-Publication Data applied for

ISBN: 1-56847-119-X

Printed in Italy

Contents

All the words that are in **bold** appear in the glossary on page 30.

Introduction

Although our planet is called the earth, it is about seven-tenths ocean and only three-tenths land. But it is on the land that human beings live, so it is of most interest to us. The land is vital for every aspect of human life. We use its **natural resources** to provide for our basic needs. These include shelter and homes, food from farming, and materials such as iron, oil, and coal, which are used for industry, transportation, and energy supplies. The land also provides inspiration for our arts and places to go for our sports and leisure activities.

If you took and airplane and flew over the world looking at the land below, you would see how humans have changed the land. You might see hedges, fields, rice paddies, or greenhouses, all of which show how people have changed the land for agriculture. Mines, quarries, and factories show how land is used for industry, while villages, towns, and cities show land use for housing and living. Transportation routes, such as canals, roads, railroads, and airports link these places together and provide a transportation network.

An aerial view of land in northern India shows how it has been changed for farming.

The planet Earth is our home. We rely mainly on the world's land for our food, shelter, and resources.

Midtown New York and not a tree in sight! Some land has been completely cleared of plant life to build settlements.

As the human population has increased and farming and technology have improved, people have had more effect on the land. In the U.S., 20 percent of all timberland has been destroyed since the nation's birth. Today about 55 percent of the earth's total land surface is heavily used by people, 30 percent is partly used, and only 15 percent is untouched or only slightly used.

Landscapes

A desert landscape is very different from a tropical rain forest – but why does the land look different in different places? There are many factors that affect the landscape. The first has to do with the structure of the earth itself.

The outer layer of the earth is called the crust, and over the four billion years since the earth was formed, the crust has moved and shifted, forming mountains, plains, and deep ocean trenches. **Glaciers** have cut through the land, and erupting volcanoes and earthquakes have torn the land apart. Rivers have worn through rocks to form valleys,

and sea levels have risen and fallen. All these events and many more have helped to shape the landscape.

The appearance of the landscape is also affected by the rock and soil that lie underneath. Soils are made very slowly, often over thousands of years, as the weather gradually breaks down rocks into finer and finer particles. Dead plants and animals also rot down into the soil. Plants need **nutrients** from the soil in order to grow, and different types of plants are suited to different types of soil. Soils from volcanic rock, for example, are very **fertile** and good for farming.

Sand dunes in a desert. Deserts are very dry regions with very little rainfall.

Wilderness

Land that lies in its natural state is called wilderness. Wilderness can be found in places all over the world, places such as tropical rain forests, Antarctic lands, or remote islands.

A wilderness has never been cleared or planted so everything that grows there is natural vegetation. Wildernesses have few people living in them, except for small numbers of local peoples – such as the South American Indians in the Amazon forest.

Wildernesses are important because they are areas that may have unique types of plant and animal life. Their **ecosystems** are

A few people live in wilderness areas such as the Amazon rain forest.

mostly untouched by humans. It is important that they stay untouched. If a wilderness is disturbed, the plant and animal life may suffer. If a wilderness is destroyed by human activity such as logging, mining, or farming, the original plants and animal life may disappear forever.

The weather also changes the landscape. The general patterns of weather are called the climate. Climates determine how fast a rock can break down into soil, how much water there is, and what plants can grow. There are wide differences in climate patterns all over the world. A forest in the tropics may receive over 80 inches of rain a year and the average temperatures may be 75°F. At the poles only 6 - 12 inches of rain falls in a year, and temperatures can drop below -22°F.

Gemsbok graze on the grasslands bordering the Kalahari Desert in Botswana, Africa.

Living things such as animals and plants also change the landscape. Plants, or **vegetation**, need soil, rain, and sunlight to grow. Different types of vegetation are suited to different types of climates. Rain forests flourish in areas that have ideal growing conditions. In the hot, wet climate plants grow fast so there are thick forests and giant trees.

The vegetation provides a home for animals, which depend on it for food and shelter. The rich rain-forest plants attract many different **species**, whereas a desert has only a few species that can survive in the dry and hot conditions.

The rocks, soil, weather, plants, and animals together make up an ecosystem in each area or region.

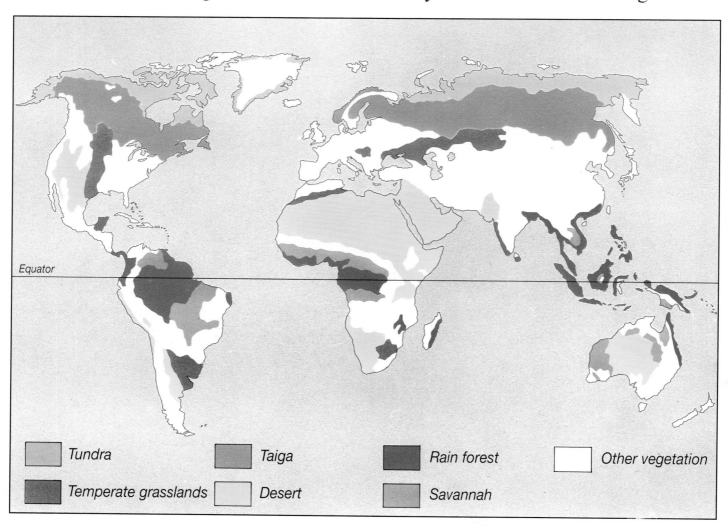

Equator

| | Tundra | | Taiga | | Rain forest | | Other vegetation |
| | Temperate grasslands | | Desert | | Savannah | | |

This map shows the main types of ecosystems in the world.

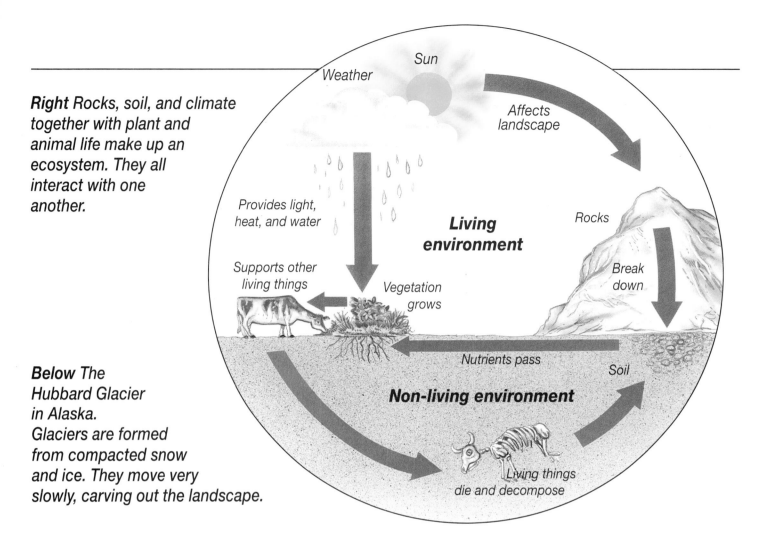

Right Rocks, soil, and climate together with plant and animal life make up an ecosystem. They all interact with one another.

Sun

Weather

Affects landscape

Provides light, heat, and water

Living environment

Rocks

Break down

Supports other living things

Vegetation grows

Nutrients pass

Soil

Non-living environment

Living things die and decompose

Below The Hubbard Glacier in Alaska. Glaciers are formed from compacted snow and ice. They move very slowly, carving out the landscape.

Everything that is a part of the ecosystem is connected, so each part affects the rest of it. Ecosystems can be small, such as a pond or piece of woodland, or large such as the world's six major types of ecosystems. These are equatorial rain forests, **savannah** grasslands, **temperate** grasslands, **taiga**, **tundra**, and hot deserts. One animal – the human being – affects the land more than any other. But people are not separate from ecosystems; they are part of them.

Food from the land

Everybody has to eat to survive, and to feed the world's 5.2 billion people, the land has to be farmed. Farming employs more people than any other occupation in the world, especially in the poorer countries. About 1 billion people – half the world's working people – are farmers or farm workers, and they provide the food for the population of the world.

Only 11 percent of the world's land surface is farmed, but wherever farming happens, the landscapes are changed. People first started to farm the land about 10,000 years ago when settlers in the fertile river basins of the Nile, Euphrates, Tigris, Ganges, and Brahmaputra in the Middle East and Asia started to grow crops and tame animals rather than hunt wild animals and gather wild plants. This was called the Agricultural Revolution.

There are several different types of farming, or agriculture.

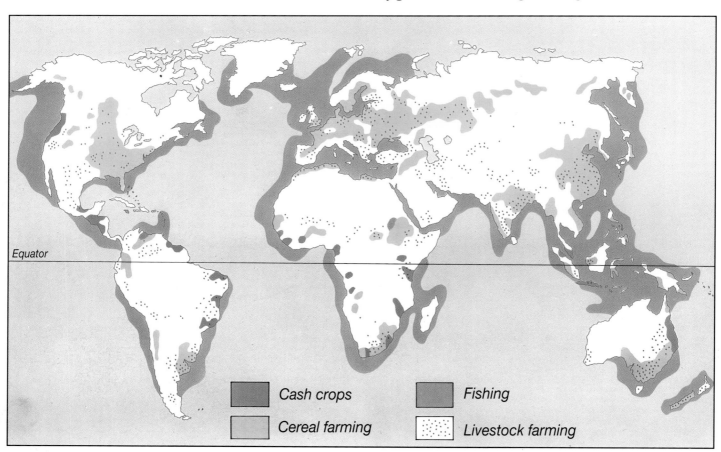

Cash crops
Cereal farming
Fishing
Livestock farming

This map shows the world's major food-growing and sea-fishing areas.

Not all land is used to produce food. These machines are harvesting cotton from an Australian field.

Arable farming means growing crops such as wheat, corn, millet, rice, and potatoes, which form the main diet of many people. These are called staple crops. Some crops are grown not to produce food, but to provide materials such as **textiles**, cooking oils, and rubber. **Livestock** farming means raising animals on pastures to provide meat, milk, leather, or wool. Cattle, pigs, sheep, goats, buffaloes, camels, and llamas are all commonly farmed.

Sheep can live on poor pasture such as this dry hillside in Sicily.

Much of the earth's surface is unsuitable for farming – it is too cold, too hot, too wet, or too dry. The landscape, soil, and climate can all determine how suitable an area is for farming. Different animals prefer different conditions. Dairy cattle need good grass, so they are usually found in fertile areas with plenty of rainfall. Sheep, goats, and pigs are hardier and can live on poorer ground, which is why sheep are sometimes kept on poorer mountains and moorland pastures. Lowland varieties of rice only grow on fertile land covered by 4 inches of water in the growing season, so there has to be plenty of water from rain or **irrigation** for this crop to survive.

Water is pumped into these rice paddies in China to provide enough water for the rice to grow.

Farms vary greatly in size. In **developing countries**, many are only a few acres, but in **developed countries**, such as the United States, there are massive wheat fields of more than 2,000 acres. Where land is in great demand and is expensive, **intensive farming** has taken over. This means raising animals indoors in stalls or cages where they take up less room. Many people feel that this type of farming is cruel to animals. Intensive crop farming usually refers to crops that are grown in greenhouses where the growing season can be controlled so it lasts longer than it would outside.

The land's resources

The land provides us with resources and materials such as metals, oil, gas, coal, timber, and rubber, which we use to make our lives easier. People have been using these valuable resources for centuries, but in the last 100 years we have been using them at a faster rate than ever before. That is because the population has grown and technology has become more complex and widespread.

Land is widely used to provide resources. Land may be used to grow trees for timber, to mine metals for industry, or to quarry stone for building. When a resource is used up, people move on to another area of land and use the resources there. Earth's resources are limited, and it takes millions of years to replace them naturally. So it makes sense not to waste resources, but to reuse or recycle them.

Rubber is just one valuable resource that the land provides. This man is tapping a tree for its rubber in Sri Lanka.

Forests cover about one-third of the earth's land, and timber is one of the world's most important resources. Humans cut down more than three billion tons of wood a year, of which about half is used as fuel for cooking and heating, mainly in developing countries. Wood is also used to build houses, make furniture, and provide wood pulp for the papermaking industry.

Forests are important because they provide **habitats** for wildlife and protect the land from **erosion** by the wind and rain. Some forests are managed so that trees are replanted to replace those felled.

Lumber is often used in buildings such as this traditional wood-framed house in Japan.

An open-cast copper mine in Queensland, Australia.

When trees are not replaced, the environment can suffer greatly.

Minerals such as iron, gold, silver, and tin are taken from rocks in the earth's crust. They are valuable because they can be used as **raw materials** for industry. Industry relies mainly on about eighty key minerals. Since people want more goods and products, the mining that is carried out all over the world increases. Some mines are underground and others are on the surface. Surface sites are called open-cast mines, and they can be extremely wide and deep.

Thousands of people traveled to California in the 1800s to find gold and make their fortune.

The Gold Rushes

Some minerals such as gold, silver, and diamonds are very valuable. In the United States, the discovery of gold in 1848 at Sutter's Mill, California, led to the gold rushes.

In 1849, 80,000 people migrated to the West hoping to make their fortune. They set up many camps and towns in this area.

There were also gold rushes to the Yukon area in Alaska.

As the gold deposits were used up, gold mining declined and so did some of the towns and camps they created. There is only one remaining large mine in the United States at Lead in South Dakota. The United States is now the world's fourth largest producer of gold.

Energy is needed to heat and light buildings, drive cars, trains, and airplanes, and to power factories. Some forms of energy sources come directly from under the ground. Coal, oil, and gas are fossil fuels that have formed over thousands of years underground. They have to be removed by mining or drilling operations. Fossil fuels are found only in some parts of the world. The Middle East, for example, has big underground reserves of coal, oil, and gas, but other places have none at all. People are always looking for new supplies of these valuable fuels. Fossil fuels can be difficult to extract from the ground, and burning them can damage the environment through air **pollution**.

A wind farm in California. These windmills generate electricity.

Today, we are trying to make use of other, renewable sources of energy such as solar power and wind power rather than fossil fuels.

Before we can make use of resources, most of them have to be processed and then manufactured into goods. The place where goods are made may be near the source of the raw material or near the market where the finished goods will be sold. If the factories are far from the markets, they will usually be near a harbor, a highway, or a railroad terminal. Sometimes local governments offer industries money to attract them to a particular area.

Places to live

In all societies across the world, people need homes for shelter. People use land and resources to build houses to live in. Groups of houses are called **settlements**.

Settlements grew as people stopped being hunter-gatherers and settled down to farm the land. As agricultural methods improved, farmers could feed more people.

This freed settlers to develop skills other than farming. Some became craftsmen and builders for example. Slowly villages grew larger and towns and cities began to develop.

Today, fertile areas with good climate have become heavily populated, while others, too hot, too cold, too steep, or too forested

A small village settlement in Kenya, Africa.

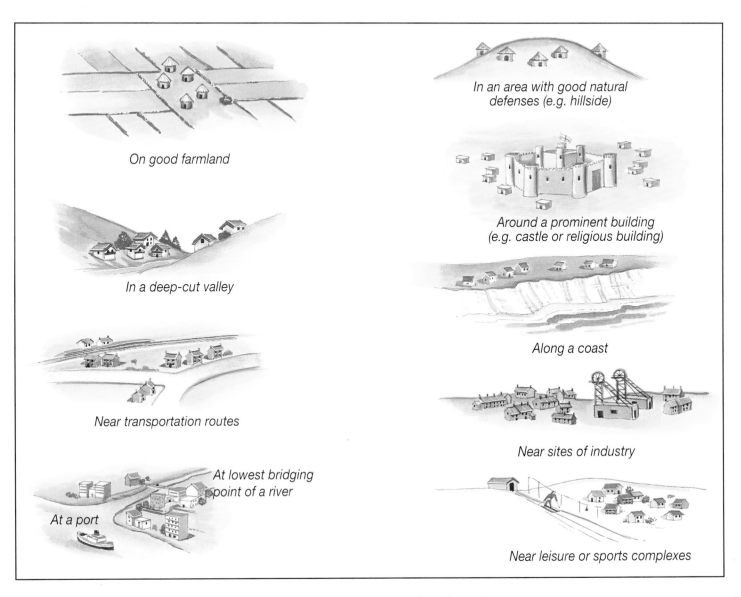

On good farmland

In a deep-cut valley

Near transportation routes

At a port

At lowest bridging point of a river

In an area with good natural defenses (e.g. hillside)

Around a prominent building (e.g. castle or religious building)

Along a coast

Near sites of industry

Near leisure or sports complexes

These are some of the locations where settlements have developed.

have few, if any, people living in them. People tend to settle where they can earn a living – maybe because the land is fertile and grows good crops, because there are mineral resources nearby, or because transportation links are good.

Settlements vary in size from isolated houses or farms in the countryside to huge cities with millions of homes. In some countries, small settlements are called villages. Villages are found in rural areas. They usually have a number of services, including stores and a school, but in some places there may be few services. The village may not even have electricity, roads, or running water. Globally, more people live in small settlements than in larger ones.

Las Vegas

The American city of Las Vegas is situated in the driest part of Nevada — the Mojave Desert.

Towns and cities are usually found near some natural resource such as a river, a mineral deposit, or a harbor, but Las Vegas in an exception. It is located in the Mojave Desert in Nevada – one of the driest and apparently most uninhabitable parts of the country. But it has a population of 250,000 and can hold up to 150,000 tourists.

The reason for the success of Las Vegas was that the state authorities decided to relax the gambling laws in 1931. This led to a steady expansion of the town with the arrival of casinos, hotels, night clubs, and restaurants. It is now a popular resort with one-third of the work force of the city employed in the tourism and entertainment industry.

After a village, the next size of settlement is a town, which is often a regional center. A town usually has stores, hotels, hospitals, movie theaters, sports centers, banks, and a post office. In some countries, such as Australia, most of the people live in towns and cities, and few live in the countryside.

Cities are larger settlements than towns, perhaps holding about one million people. A city may have a university and be an important religious, government, or commercial center. Very large cities such as London or Los Angeles are called metropolises. They may have more than one million people and have several universities, airports, national museums, art galleries, and sports stadiums, as well being the headquarters of international companies.

Hong Kong is very crowded, with a population of 5.7 million. It is an international center for trade and finance.

Transportation

In most parts of the world, people need transportation – they want to move around to get to work, to shop, or to visit friends. Transportation is also vital for the economy of a country – for moving industrial, agricultural, mining, and forestry products from where they are produced to where they are processed and sold.

Transportation networks have developed over centuries from tracks and bridlepaths, where people and animals walked, to highways, intercity rail networks, and international air travel routes.

Humans have developed the technology to build bridges to overcome natural barriers such as rivers or gorges. This is the Golden Gate Bridge in San Francisco, California.

The way that these networks have developed depends on the **terrain**. Mountains, gorges, rivers, and seas may act as barriers to road and rail; shallow waters, rapids, and waterfalls are dangerous to ships.

In the developed world, money and technology are available to overcome many natural barriers. Tunnels, bridges, harbors, and canals can be built or waterways dredged to deepen water channels.

The St. Lawrence Seaway created a trade route in the Great Lakes region of North America.

This road runs through the Brazilian rain forest and has developed farming and industry.

In the 1950s, Canada and the United States cooperated to overcome the rapids and narrow channels of the St. Lawrence River to create the St. Lawrence Seaway linking the Great Lakes with the Atlantic Ocean.

Poor countries often cannot afford to build these kinds of networks, although some governments will give money to a project to open up an area of land. In Brazil, the government has funded the building of the Trans-Amazonian Highway to attract people to the interior of the Amazon Basin and to develop farmland, forest, and mineral resources. Unfortunately, to build this road, a great many trees have been cut down in the tropical rain forest.

Good transportation networks are vital if a country wants to develop its agriculture and industry. Factories are often built along roads or railroads because this makes it easier to distribute goods.

Air travel has overcome many of the problems posed by natural barriers in the landscape – airplanes simply fly over them. Although airplanes use the air, they still use the land for runways and airport buildings. Major international airports attract many businesses and industries nearby such as catering, taxis, cargo handling, aircraft maintenance, and housing for airport staff.

Highways and railroads are important transportation networks for industry and agriculture.

Rotterdam in the Netherlands is the world's busiest port and handles most of Europe's sea trade.

Rotterdam Europoort

Rotterdam in the Netherlands is a major European port situated in the delta of the Rhine River and the Meuse River. About one-third of all the goods that are transported in the European Community pass through the port, which has good road, rail, and water links with other countries.

Some of the goods that arrive at Rotterdam are transhipped. This means that the cargo is transferred from one ship to another before sailing for another port. Barges carry the goods up inland waterways to ports such as Strasbourg in France and Basle in Switzerland. The other goods are off-loaded to trucks or trains. This has put the Netherlands in a strong position as the major freight transporter in Europe, loading and unloading millions of tons of goods each year.

Pressure on the land

Land is a valuable resource, but in many places it is under threat, especially from human activities.

Industry is important in the developed world; it provides jobs for people and supplies goods that improve our lives. We also build houses, stores, offices, parks, and leisure centers. All these things use up land, and to make way for them often means countryside is destroyed.

Trees may be felled and wetlands drained. Wildlife habitats are lost as more and more ground is covered with concrete. In the United States, for example, some studies show that farmland has disappeared at a rate of almost 500,000 acres every year through building.

Towns can sometimes grow in an uncontrolled way, called **urban sprawl**. Los Angeles, California, covers more than 450 square miles of

Extra space for living is provided by high-rise buildings and by boats in crowded Hong Kong.

Left Detergent is sprayed onto rocks polluted by an oil spill. Oil pollution may be caused by a tanker accident, but it often results when ships wash out their tanks at sea.

Below Waste litters a street in Saigon, Vietnam. Garbage can be a health hazard.

land. Three million people live there, on land that once was vineyards, orange groves, and farms. During the 1950s and 1960s, almost 3,000 acres of land a day were lost to road-building. Some cities, such as New York and Hong Kong, cannot spread out because there is no land left; instead they build upward with skyscrapers and high-rise buildings.

There is also pressure on the land from waste. Houses, stores, offices, and especially factories all create waste – whether it is the garbage that goes in the trash can or the waste from manufacturing goods in industry. If waste is not handled properly, it can cause pollution.

In some cases pollution has been so bad that the land can no longer be used. Most industries today try not to cause pollution, but things do sometimes go wrong, causing disasters.

New Land in the Netherlands

About 40 percent of the Netherlands would be under water if it had not been **reclaimed**. This new land has been created from areas of sea or wetland, or from neglected land that is now restored. The biggest project in the Netherlands was the Zuider Zee Project.

The Zuider Zee was once a large gulf of the sea, which often flooded the surrounding land. In 1927, work started on building a barrier dam that began to cut off the North Sea. Gradually the Zuider Zee became a freshwater lake instead of salty sea. Dutch engineers drained areas of the new lake, producing new land.

A new area of land in the Netherlands created by draining the Zuider Zee.

The new areas are called polders, and they are used mainly for agriculture and housing. Some land has been set aside for nature preserves, and woodlands and beaches have also been created.

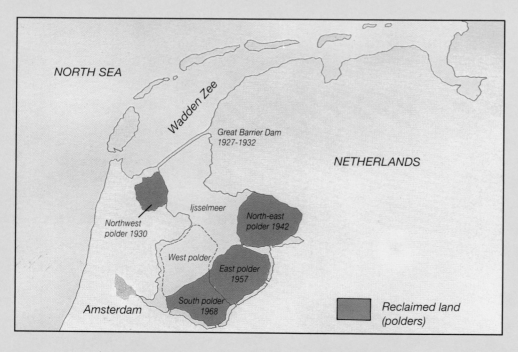

NORTH SEA

Wadden Zee

Great Barrier Dam
1927-1932

NETHERLANDS

Northwest polder 1930

Ijsselmeer

North-east polder 1942

West polder

East polder 1957

South polder 1968

Amsterdam

Reclaimed land (polders)

This diagram shows the stages of draining the Zuider Zee. The new polders are large areas of flat land drained by ditches and canals.

A lack of planning laws can lead to city sprawl and often to squatter settlements such as this shantytown in Rio de Janeiro, Brazil.

In some countries, planning departments have been set up by local and national governments to help solve the problems of overdevelopment and pollution. People who work in planning may decide how land is to be used and approve new plans for building. Planners are usually involved with housing, transportation, removal of minerals from the ground, leisure and recreation, office building, and new plans for the inner city. Planners talk to politicians and the public, as well as to architects, engineers, property developers, pressure groups, and community organizations. They make plans for an area and watch closely how the plans develop.

This has helped to save land from being badly or wrongly used in some places, but in some developing countries the rules may not be so strict, allowing settlements to grow unchecked, often without good water and sewage systems, and often in unsuitable places such as next to an industrial complex. Not every country has planners or enough planning laws and regulations to keep this from happening.

Glossary

Arable farming Planting land that has been tilled for crops such as wheat, corn, and potatoes.

Developed countries Countries that have complex systems for industry, transportation, and finance.

Developing countries Countries that rely mostly on farming, and do not yet have complicated industrial, financial, or transportation structures.

Ecosystem A community of animals and plants and the environment they live in.

Erosion The wearing away of the land by rain, rivers, ice, or wind.

Fertile Rich in material that is needed for growing plants.

Glacier A slow-moving mass of ice formed by compacted snow.

Habitat A particular area, such as a forest, in which certain plants and animals normally live.

Intensive farming Farming that aims to produce large amounts of food from a small area of land.

Irrigate To supply water to a farmland by a system of canals and pipes.

Livestock The domesticated animals that are farmed for products such as milk, eggs, meat, and wool.

Natural resources Anything useful to us that occurs in nature such as forests or minerals.

Nutrient Something that feeds or nourishes plants or animals, enabling them to grow and repair themselves.

Pollution The release of harmful substances into the air, water, or land.

Raw materials The basic materials used in making a product. (Timber is the raw material used to make wood pulp for the paper industry.)

Reclaimed land New land that has been made from areas of sea, wetland, or land that had been abandoned.

Savannah Grassland areas with hot wet and hot dry seasons that border equatorial forests. The vegetation is grass and scattered trees.

Settlement A group of houses or dwellings.

Species A group of animals or plants that can breed with one another.

Taiga Coniferous forest in the northern hemisphere.

Temperate Mild. The areas of the world found between the tropics and the polar regions have a temperate climate.

Textiles Woven materials.

Terrain The nature or the surface of the land.

Tundra The treeless plains of northern North America and northern Europe and Asia lying mainly on the Arctic circle.

Urban sprawl Towns or cities that have spread out to cover a large area.

Vegetation The plant life of a particular area or region.

Books to read

Beekman , Daniel. *Forest, Village, Town, City*. New York: HarperCollins, 1982.

Challand, Helen J. *Vanishing Forests*. Saving Planet Earth. Chicago: Childrens Press, 1991.

Chrisp, Peter. *The Farmer Through History*. Journey Through History. New York: Thomson Learning, 1993.

Davies, Eryl. *Transport: On Land, Road and Rail*. Timelines. New York: Franklin Watts, 1992.

Dixon, Dougal. *The Changing Earth*. Young Geographer. New York: Thomson Learning, 1993.

Lambert, Mark: *Farming and the Environment*. Austin: Raintree Steck-Vaughn, 1990.

Peckham, Alexander. *Changing Landscapes*. Green Issues. New York: Gloucester Press, 1991.

Willis, Teri. *Land Use and Abuse*. Chicago: Childrens Press, 1992.

Notes for activities

Choose a local area and make a land-use map. Use different symbols, colors, shadings, abbreviations, or labels to display how buildings, woods, fields, stores, services, and so on are used. Look at a detailed map of the area to see how it shows differences in land use.

Find out what industries are situated in your area. Perhaps you can discover why they were built there. Is their location a help or a disadvantage to them?

Investigate the types of land use within the school grounds. Draw a plan of your school and mark which areas are buildings, playgrounds, etc.

Study the effect of a new road, bypass, or highway in your area. What was there before? What development has taken place since? Find out what people felt about the road before and after it was built.

Study the growth of a town. Which are the oldest and newest parts? Analyze why the town has grown — perhaps due to industry, commuting, or transportation links. Devise a questionnaire and interview local people on how they feel about their town and how it has changed.

Index

Picture acknowledgments

The publishers would like to thank the following for allowing their photographs to be reproduced in this book: Bruce Coleman Ltd. 13 top (L. R. Dawson), 18 (Gerald Cubitt), 20 (Norman Tomalin); Mary Evans Picture Library 16; Jimmy Holmes 15 top; J. Allan Cash *title page*, 15 bottom, 23 top, 27 top, 28 top; Tony Stone Worldwide *front cover* (Andy Sacks), *back cover* (Roger Tully), 4 both (Anthony Cassidy left), 5, 6 (Peter Lamberti), 7 bottom (Chris Harvey), 9 (Olaf Soot), 11 top (David Austen), 12 (Margaret Gowan), 14 (Bryn Campbell), 17 (Glen Allison), 21 (Doug Armand), 22 (Glen Allison), 23 bottom (Donald Nausbaum), 24 (Hans Schlapfer), 26, 29 (Sue Cunningham); Wayland Picture Library 11 bottom, 13 bottom; Zefa 7 top, 25, 27 (bottom). Artwork is by Peter Bull.